Nap Time

Print the word seagull.

Seahorse Ride

Can you find the anchor?
Print that word.

an

Stay at the Beach

Fish mouths blow bubbles.
Print a word with an l and b in it.

_____
_____
_____

Seahorse Vacation

Print the word teamwork.

Hermit Crabs House

Color one shell orange.
Print the word orange.

Crabs Printing Words

Print the title above.
_____
=======================
_____

Swim Time

Color the heart red, and print the word swimming.

_____
_____
_____

Baby Whale

Print the word whale.

_____
=======================
_____

Computer Time

Print the word computer

_____

_____

Adventures Await

Print the word turtle.

Seagull With Sand Shovel

Print the words sand shovel.

_____

_____

Mermaid's Castle

Print the word mermaid

Octopus Castle

Print the word octopus not capatilized like the title is .

_____
_____
_____

School of Fish

Can you find a bell? Print the word bell.

bell

Little Seal

The seal likes to eat fish.
Print food you like that starts with f.

_____

_____

Stacking Rocks

Count the starfish.
Print the number of starfish.

Unicorn Whale

Look for the unicorn whale's clock.
Print the object you found. 🕐

clock

Starfish slide

Print the word slide

slide

Splish Splash

Print the word splashing.

_____
_____
_____

Friendly Fish

What is the shrimp standing on?
Print the word. It starts with the letter r.

_____

_____

Fun at the Beach

An umbrella gives shade on the beach.
Print the word that gives shade.

_____

_____

Jellyfish

Jellyfish are not made of jelly.
They are made of 95% water.
Print the word jellyfish.

Painting a Picture

Print the word painting.

_____

_____

Carrying his Castle

Spell out the three words of the title on the top of the page.

_____

_____

Nice Break

Can you print the word of what you like to drink?

_____
_____

Tying Shoes

Practice printing the number eight.
The octopus has eight legs.

Sunny Day

Its a sunny play day..
Print the word sunny.

Day Out

Find the ice cream cone.
Print the name of what you found.

_____
_____

Landed

**Pelicans can sleep standing.
Do you sleep standing, sitting, or lying?**

_____
_____
_____

Letter Game

Print out an animal that starts with z.

New hair tie

Count the pearls on her head.
Print the number below.

_____
_____

Inner Tubing

Find his goggles.
Print the object you found.

Blowfish on Computer

The blowfish loves his glasses for reading. Print the word reading.

_____

_____

Sailing

Can you find the dolphin?
Print that seven letter word.

Otter Slide

**Names start with a capital letter.
Give him a name that starts with T.**

_____
_____
_____

Shrimp

Can you find the hermit crab?

Print the two word creature you found.

_____

_____

Fish Barista

Look for the fish's cap.
Print the word cap

Tastey Treat

Seahorses are marine life. It means found in sea. Print the word marine.

_____

_____

Hermit Crab Lunchtime

Please print the word you found.
Can you find the spoon? 🥄

S

Day at the Pier

Can you find the paddle?
Print the name on the lines below.

_____

_____

Just Friends

Can you find the turtle?
Print the name of what you found.

_____

_____

Happy Birthday!

Print Happy Birthday.

_____

_____

Blue Whale

A new baby Blue Whale can weigh 5000 pounds. Print what youu weigh.

_____

_____

_____

Sail Boating

Where is the dragonfly?
Print out the insect name.

d r

Proud Starfish

The Starfish is proud of his work. Print the word proud.

_____
_____
_____

Fast Swimmer

Look for the crab. Now print that word. Letter b touches the top line.

Thristy Crab

Can you find the letter d?
Print the word drink.

_____
=======================
_____

Dophin Ride

Print below what your favorite animal is.

_____

_____

Gone Fishing

Look under the bridge.. 🐸
Find the frog and print the word.

_____

_____

Made in the USA
Columbia, SC
09 September 2024

41477958R00028